Read more about Anna and her friends
in the first three books:

The Year of the Book

A JUNIOR LIBRARY GUILD SELECTION
"A pleasure to read and more. This is a
novel to treasure and share with every
middle-grade reader you know."
—*New York Times Book Review*

The Year of the Baby

A JUNIOR LIBRARY GUILD SELECTION
★ "This book deals deftly with a range
of thorny adoption—and ethnic—
stereotyping issues."
—*SLJ,* starred review

"Anna continues to be a perceptive
and intelligent narrator, with an observational eye that is
genuine, sensitive, and astute." —*The Bulletin*

The Year of the Fortune Cookie

A JUNIOR LIBRARY GUILD SELECTION
"This is just right for middle-grade Anna
fans ready for new experiences."
—*Kirkus Reviews*

"Fans of Anna's previous adventures will
definitely want to keep following her as she
journeys toward young adulthood."
—*The Bulletin*

The Year of the Three Sisters

* AN ANNA WANG NOVEL *

by Andrea Cheng

illustrations by Patrice Barton

Houghton Mifflin Harcourt
Boston New York

www.hmhco.com

The text of this book is set in ITC Berkeley Oldstyle.

Library of Congress Cataloging-in-Publication Data
Cheng, Andrea.
The year of the three sisters / by Andrea Cheng ; illustrated by Patrice Barton.
p. cm.
Sequel to: Year of the fortune cookie.
Summary: Twelve-year-old Anna's friend Andee spearheads a campaign to bring
Fan from China to Cincinnati on a year-long cultural exchange, but before Fan even
arrives Anna is concerned that Andee and Fan are too different to get along.
ISBN 978-0-544-34427-3
1. Chinese Americans—Juvenile fiction. [1. Chinese Americans—Fiction.
2. Friendship—Fiction. 3. Foreign study—Fiction.] I. Barton, Patrice, 1955–
illustrator. II. Title.
PZ7.C41943Yk 2015
[Fic]—dc23
2014013599

Manufactured in the United States of America
DOC 10 9 8 7 6 5 4 3 2 1
4500522504

To the Wu family
   —A.C.

To Lily
   —P. B.

Contents

CONTENTS

PRONUNCIATION GUIDE

Sun - *Tai yang (Tie yang)* 太阳

Hot - *Re (re)* 热

Yellow - *Huang se (hwang se)* 黄色

Melon - *Gua (gwa)* 瓜

Playground - *You le chang (yo le chang)* 游乐场

Ice Cream - *Bing qi ling (bing ji ling)* 冰淇淋

Welcome - *Huan ying (hwan ying)* 欢迎

How was your flight? - *Lu shang zen me yang*

　　(loo shang ze me yang) 路上怎么样

Good - *Hao (how)* 好

Thank you - *Xie xie (shay shay)* 谢谢

Very tired - *Tai Lei Le (tie lay le)* 太累了

Grandfather (mother's side) - *Wai gong (why gong)* 外公

　　or *Gong Gong (gong gong)* 公公

Grandmother (mother's side) - *Wai po (why po)* 外婆
  or *Po Po* 婆婆

Badminton - *Yu mao qiu (oo mao chio)* 羽毛球

Sorry - *Dui bu qi (duay bu chi)* 对不起

Residence permit - *Hu kou (Hu ko)* 户口

Goodbye - *Zai jian (zsai jian)* 再见

Sister (older) - *Jie jie (je je)* 姐姐

Dad - *Ba ba (ba ba)* 爸爸

Chapter One

A Plan

$\mathcal{M}$y mom doesn't believe in air conditioning. It's not healthy, she says, to go from hot to cold. So I stand in front of the window fan, waving my shirt to dry the sweat.

I sit down at my desk and reread the letter that came yesterday from Fan, my waitress friend in China.

Dear Anna,
I am sorry it takes me so long to answer. Thank you for telling me about the presentation to your school. I am embarrassed that you present me but I am proud too. In your last

letter you ask about my summer. Summer season the hotel is very busy so there are many tables to clean and now I am a cooker in the kitchen too. You ask how is my brother. He is fine. He plays all day but I give him homework so he can be a good student, better than me. My mother is fine but my father hurt from his job (his back). He is builder and the materials are very heavy. Sorry I cannot explain in English. I hope you understand.

I will give you a small Chinese lesson with summer season words:

Sun - tai yang

太阳

Hot - re

热

Yellow color - huang ze

黄色

Melon - gua

瓜

Playground - you le chang

游乐场

Ice cream - bing ji ling

冰淇淋

Please send me English lesson. I still dream to learn English more. Then I can work better in the hotel like at the desk in the lobby. That is the word in my dictionary. Is it correct?

Now I am tired. Thank you, my friend.

Yours truly,

Fan

PS: Here is my try poem in English:

You are my friend

Far away

But sun rises in East

Goes away in West

We are one world,
Sisters.

I love the way Fan calls her verse a *try poem.* I open the small photo album I put together after my trip to China this past December. The last page has a picture of Fan the day I left, wearing her waitress uniform and smiling shyly at the camera. I look more closely at her face, but it's impossible to tell what she is thinking. Fan asked me lots of questions about America, and she loved looking at photos of my family. She said she would like to visit, but then when I asked her if she could really come someday, she said, *For you it is easy to get on an airplane. But for me it is not possible.*

I take a sheet of paper out of my desk drawer:

Dear Fan,
Thank you for your letter. I really like your poem. I wish I could write that well in Chinese.
In the morning I am helping my teacher

take care of the baby she adopted in China.

The phone rings and I go into the hallway to answer it. "Hey, Anna." Andee's deep voice is so different from everyone else's I know.

"I thought you were still in Vermont!"

"I came back a week early. Can I come over?"

Andee is suntanned and her curly hair is lighter than before. She has on long boy shorts and a green T-shirt, and she looks taller. She hugs me, and we head up to my room. When I ask Andee about Vermont, she says, "My grandparents enrolled me in this outdoor adventure thing, which was fine, but the kids . . . I don't know, I just felt like I didn't have anything in common with anyone."

"So you left early?"

Andee nods, then reaches for her backpack. "I brought you something." She hands me a tiny bottle of Genuine Vermont Maple Syrup.

I hold the bottle up so it catches the sunlight. "How did you know I love miniature things?"

Andee smiles. "Just a guess. What were you doing when I called?"

"Writing back to my friend in China." I show Andee the letter from Fan, and her eyes move quickly over the words.

"So while I was climbing mountains with a bunch of rich teenagers, your friend was cleaning tables in a hotel." Andee sees the photo of Fan. "We're almost the same age, aren't we?"

"She's a year older, I think."

"A sophomore?"

"She had to drop out after eighth grade." As soon as I say the word "drop out," I think of kids who fail their classes. "Fan had to leave school to earn money for her family," I explain.

"I wish we could give them the money my grandparents wasted on that adventure camp." Andee turns to me. "Hey, maybe Fan could go to high school here for a year. Then she'd really learn English."

It's hard for me to imagine Fan in the front hallway at Fenwick High School, surrounded by American students. The only places she has ever been, she told me, are Beijing and the small village where she was born. "Fan could never afford the plane ticket," I say, remembering what she said about traveling. "Her family is . . ." I don't want to say "poor" because I don't really know what poor means in China. "They don't earn a lot of money."

Andee takes a deep breath. "I bet my parents and my grandparents would donate. Plus the Community Action Team is always looking for projects. And living here would be practically free. She could stay in one of our guest rooms." Once Andee gets an idea, she cannot stop talking. "I forgot to tell you: my mom joined the Local School Decision-Making Committee, and she convinced them to offer Mandarin Chinese at Fenwick High starting in September. We were planning to host an exchange student from China anyway, so this would be perfect!"

Andee is always so sure that she can make things work out. "Fan's family needs the money she earns at the hotel," I say. "Her parents don't earn very much, and they have to send money to her grandparents in the countryside every week."

Andee pulls her eyebrows together. "We could set up one of those donor pages online. It's a really good cause."

"Fan isn't exactly a 'cause.'" My voice comes out louder than I expected.

Andee looks at me. "You know what I mean."

I wipe my face with my T-shirt. I think the heat is getting to me. I feel bad for snapping at Andee when she is just trying to help my friend. Fan did tell me that if she knew English better, she could probably get promoted at the hotel and help her family more. Maybe, if we can pay for everything, Andee's plan really could work out.

"I can't wait to tell my mom," Andee says as we head downstairs to get a snack. "She's really good at arranging things. "

While we eat our ice cream, we talk about all the things we could do with Fan if she comes: take her to the zoo, to King's Island, or the swimming pool if it's still as hot as it is now.

It's after eleven, but I can't sleep. China is thirteen hours ahead, so it's just after noon there. Fan is probably at the hotel, setting the tables for lunch. Or maybe she is taking a break and studying the English vocabulary that I wrote down in her notebook. Fan told me that even though she left school in eighth grade, she would never stop trying to learn. I know that the best way to learn a language is to be surrounded by it. I learned more Chinese in two weeks in China than I did in two years at Chinese school. So why does my stomach flip when I imagine Fan in Cincinnati?

I move to a cool spot on the bed. How would Fan feel in Andee's house, where each room is bigger than her whole apartment? In China, she lives in an alley with lots of other migrant families. They all share a public bathroom, and they cook on electric hot plates or small charcoal grills that line the street. Andee's house has a bathroom for each person, and a stove with six burners.

I sit up and look out the window. Last year Andee and I had so much fun planning our CAT projects together. But today I notice her insistence more, as if everything has to happen exactly the way she thinks it should. Andee is older than me by two years, but she has never been to China and she doesn't know anything about Fan's life. Of course, after two weeks,

I don't know that much either. Still, I talked to Fan almost every day I was there, and we ate dumplings in the small room that she shares with her parents and her brother.

I lie back down with my arms crossed behind my head. I miss Camille. She spends every summer in Oklahoma with her grandparents, but this time it seems as if she's been gone forever.

Chapter Two

An Invitation

After Andee's orthodontist appointment, her mom drops her off at my house. She starts talking even before she's inside the front door. "It turns out that in order to be an exchange student, you have to be enrolled in high school, and you said Fan isn't. Then my mom contacted someone she knows in D.C., and there's a way Fan can come as part of a cultural exchange program, so the lady sent us the application and my mom's working on it right now."

The idea of sending in an application without telling Fan worries me. "Don't you think we should talk to Fan first?"

"These applications can take a while to process, so

my mom thought we should get started right away." Andee covers her mouth with her hand. "My teeth are killing me."

I put a few ice cubes into a washcloth and Andee holds them to her gums. "Let's send an email to Fan," she says.

"She doesn't have a computer." I pause. "But I think she does go to Internet cafés sometimes."

Andee looks over my shoulder as I type:

Dear Fan,

I hope you and your family are doing well. I think about the time I spent in China all the time. Thank you for helping me so much while I was there.

My friend Andee and I were talking, and we have an idea. We want to invite you to come to visit us in Cincinnati. We know the airplane ticket is very expensive, but Andee's parents were planning to invite a student from China anyway, and I know you are the perfect person! You could help Andee learn Chinese and we could help you improve in English. Andee's parents would be happy to pay for the airplane ticket and you can stay at her house for free.

"Is the exchange for a year?" I ask.

"It can be for six months or nine months. But nine months would be better."

You can stay here for nine months and you can go to Fenwick High School with Andee (she is two years older than me).

Andee sucks on her ice cube. "Maybe we should tell her that the passport and visa might take a while, so she'd better start right away."

> Please tell us what you think asap (as soon as possible) because you will need a passport and a visa to come, and the application might take a long time.

Then I add,

> We hope everything works out. Just thinking about you in Cincinnati makes me excited! I miss you!
> Yours,
> Anna and Andee

As soon as I click "Send" I realize that I haven't asked my parents.

"They don't really have to do anything," Andee says. "If Fan lives with us and my mom applies for the cultural exchange, there isn't anything your parents have to arrange."

Andee is right. My parents don't know anything

about exchange programs, and they don't have money to buy tickets and pay for applications. But I still feel as if my family should be included. I get an ice cube out of the freezer and hold it to my forehead.

"We should start figuring out how to raise money," Andee says. "We could do a 5K walk. I bet people would pledge."

I think of the walks I've done for cancer and AIDS. A walk for Fan makes it seem like somebody is sick, but I can't think of anything better. Andee writes *5K Walk* on top of a list she calls *Fan's Fund*.

By the time Andee's mom comes to get her, she has added a car wash, a plant sale, and a babysitting service.

Kaylee is running a fever, so Mom had to leave work to pick her up at daycare. When they come in, Kaylee's cheeks are red and her eyes are watery.

"Kaylee Bao Bao," I say, reaching for my sister, but she turns away. Mom gives her a drink of water and then lays her down in her crib. She hugs her sock mouse and we tiptoe out of her room.

I follow Mom into the basement, where we sort the laundry. "Light or dark?" I ask, holding up one of Ken's shirts that is white and blue striped.

"Your choice," Mom says.

I toss it into the darks. Mom puts the clothes into the washer, adds the detergent, and turns on the machine.

"I wonder if Fan's family uses a washing machine," I say.

"In China, many people wash clothes by hand," Mom says. "Especially a migrant family probably does not have money for a laundromat."

Mom is about to go back upstairs when I say, "Andee's family invited Fan to come to Cincinnati for the school year."

Mom looks surprised. "That is very nice of them. Will they pay for the ticket?"

I nod. "Andee's mom is filling out the application for a cultural exchange."

Mom sits down on the old sofa next to the dryer and motions for me to sit next to her. "That will be a very special experience for Fan," she says. "Most young

people in China don't have such an opportunity. Es-pecially migrant children."

Then for no reason at all, I feel choked up. I tell Mom how Andee is arranging everything before we even know if Fan wants to come. "I'm not sure Fan will like it here," I say, remembering the parks full of people in Beijing and the buses that go everywhere.

Mom pulls me close and I feel her dry hands

smoothing my hair. "There are things she would like and things she would not like," Mom says. "Just like in China. There were things that you liked and things that you didn't like, right?"

"I didn't like the toilets because they were only holes in the ground," I say. "But I liked riding the bus everywhere."

"When I first came to the U.S., I thought the food tasted funny," Mom says.

"What did you like?"

"The way everyone stops at red lights. The drivers in China don't pay attention to the rules." I can feel mom's shoulder against mine.

"Fan will be lonely at Andee's house. It's so big that you don't even hear other people."

"A house is a house, Anna. And Mr. and Mrs. Wu are very generous." Mom looks out the small basement window. "If Fan wants to stay with us sometimes, there is always room." The basement is cool, and Mom pulls an afghan around our shoulders. "First we have to see if her parents will let her. Sometimes Chinese parents are very protective and also they don't want to impose on other people. I will write Fan's mother a letter in Chinese. From one mother to another. That is important."

"What will you say?"

We watch our clothes churning in the washer—my jeans, Ken's striped T-shirt, Kaylee's red dress with white hearts. "I will tell her that in America, her daughter is my daughter," Mom says.

"And Andee and I are her American sisters," I add.

Mom sits at the dining room table with a legal pad and writes a letter to Fan's mother. She covers the page with perfect Chinese characters, and then she recopies it before putting it into an envelope.

"Do you have the address?" she asks.

I try to imagine a mail carrier delivering letters in the alley where Fan lives. Each room must have a number, but it seems as if it would be very hard to figure out where everyone lives. "Maybe we should send it to the hotel."

I run to get the address and Mom copies it neatly onto the envelope.

Chapter Three
A Reply

$\mathcal{E}$very morning I check the email, but there is no reply from Fan. Finally on Monday morning, I see her name in my inbox.

Dear Anna,

Thank you very much to you and your friend for invite me and offer to buy my ticket, but I cannot come. I don't tell my mother and father. They don't leave Beijing and I go to America? But I dream about it every day.

I am tired from my job now.

*Good bye and thank you very much for think
about me.
Your friend, Fan*

My stomach drops. Fan's note is so short. She doesn't say that she will try to find a way to visit someday or that she got the letter from Mom. She doesn't write a poem or send a Chinese lesson. Did our invitation hurt her feelings in some way? At first I wasn't sure about the whole idea of inviting Fan to America, but now that she has said no, I feel so disappointed.

I call Andee and read her Fan's note over the phone. She doesn't say anything for so long that I wonder if we got disconnected. "Can you come over?" she asks finally.

"I have to babysit this morning. I'll see if my dad can bring me later."

When I get to Andee's house, she shows me earrings she is making out of shells that she found on the beach at Cape Cod. "You should get your ears pierced," she says.

"I hate needles," I say. "Even allergy shots."

"Let's make bracelets." Andee turns to face me. "I think Fan should at least have asked her parents."

Andee doesn't seem to understand that in China, helping your family is the most important thing in your life. I pick black, blue, and green thread to make a bracelet for Camille. "Maybe Fan was embarrassed to ask. To her family, going to America must sound completely impossible."

Andee is listening hard with her head tilted, the way she always did at the CAT meetings. "Are you . . . Do you think there's a still a chance that she could come?"

"My mom wrote a letter to her mom," I say. "I'm not sure if it got there yet." Andee is braiding red, pink, and white thread. Her fingers are long and agile, and the sun is shining on her hair. "I think it could make a difference."

"Anyway, Fan might not even show the letter to her parents," Andee says.

"The letter is to her mom. I think she will show it to her."

Andee takes a deep breath. "If Fan can't come, my mom said we could apply to host a regular Chinese exchange student through AFS."

Maybe Andee doesn't really care who comes as long as she has someone. We finish our bracelets without saying much.

Then Andee shows me two possible guest rooms for the exchange student, a bigger one that faces the front of the house and a smaller one in back. Both rooms have their own bathroom attached.

"If Fan ends up coming, could she share your room? In China, she shares a room with her whole family."

"Don't you think she'd want some privacy?" Andee asks.

I shake my head. "She's used to having people around all the time."

We go back into Andee's room. "There isn't really that much space in here," she says, even though her room is big. "I guess she could use the art spot, and I could move my earrings and art stuff into the guest room."

We spend the afternoon cleaning up the alcove. We take all the art supplies into the guest room and move a bed from the guest bedroom into the art alcove. I think we should ask Andee's parents first, but she says that it's her room and she's allowed to rearrange things the way she wants. "What should we put on the wall?" she asks.

"In her room, Fan has posters of flowers and Chinese movie stars." I try to think of what else we could do. "It needs something colorful."

Andee gets out a stack of origami paper. We write *Welcome* in English and *Huan ying* in Chinese on red sheets.

欢迎

Then we look on the Internet to find the words for *welcome* in other languages and copy them as best we can onto different-colored pieces of paper. By the time

Dad comes to pick me up, the alcove is full of international floating Welcome signs.

When we pull up in front of the house, Mom runs out to the car. "Anna, your friend just called from China. I talked to her mother. She said they were so happy to read my letter, and that if Mrs. Wu can arrange everything, they will allow Fan to come! I didn't want to talk for a long time because I know it's expensive. But I told her how happy we are and that we will communicate through email."

Right away I call Andee, and we have the longest phone conversation we've ever had. We talk about what classes Fan will take at Fenwick and what clubs she might join. "We can have sleepovers on the weekends," Andee says. "At either your house or mine."

I try to remember what Fan likes. "She loves ice cream."

"We can go to Graeter's and get double scoops at least once a week!" Andee says.

I turn off my light at eleven, but I feel wide awake. I can't tell if I'm nervous or excited or both. Maybe Fan should live with us. She knows me already, and Fenwick Middle School and Fenwick High are right next to each other. But Andee definitely wants an exchange student at her house. Anyway, her family has done almost everything to bring Fan here. They've spent a lot of money and made all the arrangements, and we already have the room ready. Plus Fan and Andee are closer in age. I try to imagine them next to each other. Fan is short, Andee is tall. Fan has straight black hair, Andee's is brown and curly. Fan seems older than Andee in some ways, and she is, but Andee is much more sophisticated in the way she dresses and talks. They seem really different from each other. What if they don't get along?

Chapter Four

Arrival!

Fan gets approved for the cultural exchange. Andee's parents pay for the passport and visa, and her mom calls her friend in D.C. to make sure that the applications are processed quickly. We email Fan with the details, and then Mrs. Wu buys Fan's airplane ticket for August 31. Fan will have a few days to adjust before the school year starts.

"What do you think will make Fan feel the most welcome?" Andee asks.

"Chinese food," I say.

Andee's mom takes us to the Asian market and we buy dried black mushrooms, bamboo shoots, braised gluten, and short grain rice. "Fan likes candy," I remember, so we buy a bag of Chinese lemon drops. We put all the food into their pantry.

"Anything else?" Andee asks.

"She likes poetry," I say.

We look through the books on Andee's shelf and take out *A Child's Garden of Verses*. "I used to love these poems when I was younger," Andee says.

"I still like them," I say. "Especially the one about the shadow."

"I have a little shadow that goes in and out with me," Andee says.

"And what can be the use of him is more than I can see," I say.

"He is very, very like me from the heels up to the head," Andee says.

"And I see him jump before me, when I jump into my bed!" we say together.

We put the book on a small table by Fan's bed. Then together we write a welcome poem:

Huan ying, **welcome**

欢迎

to our homes.
America and China
are on two sides of the earth.
But now you have two sisters
in America.

I copy it in my best handwriting and we tape it to the wall above Fan's bed, right in the middle of the floating Welcome signs.

Mom and I go to the airport with Andee and her parents.

"Thank you for arranging everything," Mom says to Mrs. Wu in the car. "This is such a big opportunity for Anna's friend."

"Really, it is an honor for us," Andee's mother says. "I'm so glad everything worked out."

We take the Suspension Bridge across the Ohio River, and I look out the window at the rolling hills of Northern Kentucky. Alongside the highway are fields of corn, all yellow in the late-August sun. What if Fan gets homesick like I did in China? I was only there for

two weeks, but there were times when I would have done anything to be in my own bed. I know she is older than me, but I don't think she has ever lived away from her family. What if she feels lonely in Andee's big house? I glance over at Andee, and she is fiddling with her earring.

At the airport, we stand by the rope. Each time someone young and Asian walks toward us, Andee looks at me and I shake my head. Finally, when we're about to check to see if Fan missed her connection in New York, I see a short person carrying a big bag.

"Fan!" I shout, wishing I could run past the barrier. She looks around, sees me, and hurries to meet us.

Fan is wearing an orange T-shirt that makes her skin look pale, and there are dark circles under her eyes. She shakes everyone's hand. "I am Fan," she says. "Pleased to meet you." We head toward the baggage claim.

"How was your flight?" Andee asks. Her words run together when she talks, and Fan doesn't understand.

"Lu shang zen me yang," Mom translates.

Fan nods. *"Hao."* Then she says something long and fast that I think means she couldn't sleep all night because the plane was too noisy.

Fan and Andee are standing next to each other, watching the suitcases tumble onto the conveyor belt. Fan is shorter than I remember, especially compared to Andee. And her baggy T-shirt makes her look much younger than she is. After a while Fan points to one of the suitcases. Andee's father picks it up, and we follow the signs to the parking lot.

In the car, Fan puts her head back against the seat and closes her eyes. I remember the taxi ride to the hotel when we first arrived in China. I was so tired from jet lag that I literally couldn't keep my eyes open.

❄   ❄   ❄

Andee and I take Fan upstairs and show her the bed in the art alcove. "So beautiful," she says, when she sees the room. "So big. You sleep here?" She points to Andee's bed.

"This is Andee's house," I say slowly. "I live in another house."

Fan looks out the window to the woods in the backyard. "Where is your house?"

"That way," I say, pointing. "Twenty minutes."

"Twenty minutes walking?" Fan asks.

"Driving," I say.

She points to the Welcome signs on the wall. "I like it." Then in Chinese she says, "Andee's bed is very big. You can share the bed with your friend."

I think for a minute. I could probably stay over at Andee's tonight, but maybe it would be better if Fan and Andee got to know each other. Plus, I have to babysit for Jing in the morning. "I have to go home," I say.

Fan looks disappointed. Then she rubs her face with her hands and switches back to English. "I have a gift."

She unzips her suitcase and takes out two identical blouses embroidered with birds and flowers for Andee and me, a kite for my brother, and a little blue dress for Kaylee. She also brought painted fans for Andee's parents and for mine, and calendars with pictures of Beijing for each family.

"*Xie xie*," I say.

"Thank you," Andee says, holding up the blouse.

"Try it," Fan says.

Andee looks at me. "I'll try it on later," she says.

I put the blouse on over my T-shirt. "It fits," I say, turning around so Fan can see the back.

Fan smiles. "Thank you for invite me to America." Then, right in front of us, she changes into her pajamas. "*Hen lei*," she says, yawning.

"She's tired," I say.

Fan lies down on the bed and closes her eyes. Andee and I go downstairs.

Mom has to get to the hospital by six, so she stands up to leave. "Thank you again, and call us if you need anything."

Mrs. Wu nods. "We are very excited. It will certainly be an interesting experience for all of us." She walks us to the door. "I forgot to ask, what do you think Fan would like for breakfast?"

"In China, sometimes we have noodles or rice," Mom says.

"That's easy enough," Mrs. Wu says.

"Can you spend the night?" Andee asks me. Her face looks really worried.

"I have to babysit at eight thirty."

Andee turns to her mom. "I would be glad to drive you there in the morning," Mrs. Wu says.

Andee lends me a toothbrush and pajamas that have green frogs all over them. We play a few games of cards, and then we tiptoe into her room. Fan is asleep, facing the wall.

"Maybe you should sleep on the side closer to her," Andee says, "in case she wakes up in the middle of the night."

I lie down close to the edge of the mattress and pull up the sheet.

Andee lies on her back with her arms crossed behind her head. "This is the first time in my life I've shared my room with anyone."

I think of all the times Ken has slept in my room. Even now, whenever there is a storm, he comes across the hall and curls up on my bed. I rub his back until I can feel his muscles relax. And my friend from down the street, Laura, used to spend the night at our house sometimes.

"What about when your cousin comes?" I ask.

"She sleeps in the guest room."

"When you were little, did you go to your parents' bed when there were thunderstorms?"

Andee shakes her head. "I've always loved storms. Actually, I really like being alone. I guess I'm used to it." Andee turns to me. "I'm nervous."

"About what?"

She lowers her voice. "I hope Fan likes it here."

I'm not sure what to say. "I think she will," I whisper finally.

Andee is staring at the ceiling and I wonder if she wishes she were all alone in her room right now.

❄ ❄ ❄

The clock says three thirty. Fan is sitting up in bed, holding a tiny light that looks like a pen and writing in a notebook.

"Fan," I whisper.

She looks startled.

"I decided to stay here tonight." I slide off the high mattress and go over to her bed so that our talking doesn't disturb Andee.

"Did I wake you up?" Fan asks in Chinese.

"I was already awake."

"I can't sleep more," she says, switching to English.

"You have jet lag," I say. "Like I did when I went to China."

Fan writes *jet lag* in her notebook. Then she shows me a journal entry, which she has written in English:

> My trip to America is very good. I sit next to a nice American lady with two daughters. They are half Chinese like Anna's friend Andee. Now I stay at Andee's house. I am

happy because I have two new friend sisters,
Anna and Andee. They write a welcome poem
on the wall.

Fan copied our poem into the notebook.

"Your writing is very good," I say.

"I cannot understand when Andee talks," Fan whispers.

"She talks fast," I say. "You'll get used to it."

Then Fan shows me a book of Chinese poems that

she brought. "A gift from my teacher." She opens the book to the title page, which has a handwritten note.

"What does it say?"

Fan tries to translate the note for me. "Never — never to stop." Fan searches for the right English words. "Never stop to try," she whispers.

"Never give up," I say.

Fan writes *give up* in her notebook.

Andee turns over in her sleep. Fan puts her finger to her lips, picks up *A Child's Garden of Verses,* and lies back down. I tiptoe back to Andee's bed, climb onto the high mattress, and pull the blanket up to my neck. I am grateful for the air conditioning in Andee's house, but now it feels freezing and I wish I were home.

Chapter Five

First Day in America

In the morning Andee sleeps late, and Fan and I get dressed as quietly as we can. Fan slips a shapeless dress over her head. "Good for summertime," she says.

"Did you sleep well?" Mrs. Wu asks us when we come downstairs.

"I had . . ." Fan is thinking. "Lag jet," she says.

Andee's mother smiles. "Jet lag."

"Yes, jet lag," Fan repeats.

We have noodles for breakfast, and then Andee's mom takes us to the Sylvesters' to babysit for Jing.

"We are so happy that you could come to America," Ms. Sylvester says, taking Fan's hand. "You helped us so much in China. Thank you." We play with Jing for a while. Then she gives me ten dollars and tells us to put the baby in the stroller and go buy ice cream to celebrate Fan's arrival.

The air is warm and windy, as if it might rain. On the way, Fan looks around at everything. "America is quiet," she says in Chinese.

"It is quiet here," I say. "But big cities like New York are very noisy."

Fan nods. "Here is like the countryside. When I was a little girl, I lived with my grandparents, and in the morning it was very quiet." She smiles. "Except our rooster was noisy. My grandfather Gong Gong said that the rooster was talking to me."

"Here there are no roosters," I say.

When we get to Graeter's Ice Cream Shop, I get chocolate almond, and Fan chooses peanut butter. I hold Jing up so she can see the flavors. She points to strawberry.

"I want to meet your family," Fan says.

"Soon," I say, looking at my watch.

On the way back to the Sylvesters', we stop paying attention to Jing, and by the time we get there, she has ice cream all over her face, her shirt, and the stroller. Fan looks concerned. "Your teacher is not happy," she says.

"It's no problem," I say. "We can wash everything."

Ms. Sylvester takes a picture of Jing before we get

her undressed and stick her into the bathtub. By the time Dad comes to get us, Jing is wearing clean red overall shorts and Fan has fixed her hair into three sticking-up ponytails that Jing loves.

"Just like my little brother," Fan says when she meets Ken. She puts her hands to the sides of her head to show us that they both have big ears.

"Hey, my ears aren't that big," Ken says.

"Compared to mine they are." I put my hair back to show him.

Mom says Camille called while we were at the Sylvesters'. They are back from Oklahoma, and her mother is bringing her over. Soon the three of us are playing cards in the living room.

In Chinese, Fan says Camille is very tall. "Not like most Chinese."

"My father is tall," Camille says in Chinese.

"You play basketball?" Fan asks.

Camille explains that she likes a lot of sports, especially volleyball and track.

"You can speak Chinese very well," Fan says.

"I was actually born in China," Camille explains. "But we moved to America when I was six."

"I'm not good at Chinese or sports," I say, switching to English.

"I thought you liked badminton," Camille says.

Fan does not understand, so Camille translates.

Fan smiles. "I like badminton. We play this game a lot in China."

We go down to the basement to find the rackets and the birdie. We don't have a net, but Fan, Camille, Ken, and I hit the birdie around in the front yard, trying to see how many times we can rally before the birdie hits the ground. Fan is much better than the rest of us, and she doesn't seem at all bothered by the heat. After a while, we sit in the shade of the apple tree in the front yard to take a break, and Laura walks by.

"This is Fan," I say. "We met in China, and she's going to spend the school year in America."

Fan stands up and shakes Laura's hand. Then Laura says she has to go to her mom's office. "I'm helping her out this summer. But I hope to see you soon. Are you going to Fenwick High?"

Fan doesn't understand, so I answer for her. "She's a sophomore."

After Laura leaves, Camille and I teach Fan the words *freshman, sophomore, junior,* and *senior.* She repeats them over and over again.

Mom has made stir-fried chicken and tofu, which Fan loves. She says the food in America tastes different from the food in China, but both are very good.

"Do you have pizza in China?" Ken asks.

Fan nods. "In Beijing, there is Pizza Hut."

"Then I'm going," Ken says, smiling.

After dinner, Fan yawns. "I am very tired," she says.

Mom gives her a pillow and a light blanket. She lies down on the sofa and in about five minutes, she is asleep.

Camille and I go up to my room so we won't disturb Fan. "How was Oklahoma?" I ask, grabbing a deck of cards off my dresser.

"Pretty good." We sit close together on the oval rug, and I deal the cards. "My grandparents always spoil me. But I have bad news. My parents want me to go to Springer School next year."

"You mean the school for kids with learning disabilities?"

Camille nods. "They said it's just for a year." Her voice breaks. "And then I can go back to Fenwick."

I know I should comfort Camille. I should tell her that she'll probably like Springer, and that a year will go by fast. But I can hardly hold back my tears. I helped Camille all last year and the year before, and she passed all her classes with B's and C's. And now I will be alone in the Fenwick cafeteria. I know people through CAT, but Andee and Sam have moved on to high school, and the rest of the kids aren't really my friends.

"For sure?" I ask, finally.

Camille nods. "They already put down the deposit. I tried to tell my parents to let me stay at Fenwick one more year to see if I can bring my grades up." Camille is tracing the braids of the rug. "But in Oklahoma, they had me tested, and I really . . ." Camille looks up. "It's like there are wires crossed in my brain or something. I'm not like you, Anna. Before every little quiz I get really bad stomachaches. And when we have a new assignment, I can't sleep all night." She swallows. "No matter how much I study, I'm lucky if I get C's on most of my tests."

I feel the tears come to my eyes. I knew Camille was having a hard time with school. But it seemed to me as if she was always worrying for nothing. Maybe if I had helped her more . . .

"One year is not that long," Camille whispers. "And we'll be together every Saturday in Chinese school."

In sixth grade, Laura switched to Our Lady of Angels. She said we would still see each other since we're neighbors, and we do run into each other like we did today, but she has a lot of homework and new friends. When we do get together, sometimes it's hard to know what to talk about. I know I should tell Camille that everything will be okay, that of course we will stay friends forever, but the lump in my throat is so big, I can hardly talk.

Camille shuffles the cards. "I made a calendar to count down the days until I can go back to Fenwick."

"How many?"

"Three hundred and eighty," she says.

I swallow hard.

"You'll probably be really busy with Fan," Camille says finally.

"She's staying with Andee."

"I know, but still."

We are quiet then, with only the noise of the fan to fill up the space.

Chapter Six

School

At four thirty in the morning, I hear Mom leave for work. I try to go back to sleep, but after tossing and turning for half an hour, I decide to get up. I was planning to wear my new yellow T-shirt to school on the first day, but in the near dark it looks too bright. I take the old gray one out of my drawer, get dressed, and go down to the kitchen.

Mom always wants us to eat a good breakfast, but after three bites of dry cereal, I can't eat any more. What will I do at school without Camille? I won't have anyone to wait for me in the morning or sit next to me at lunch. And with Andee at the high school, I won't have anyone to wave to in the hallway either.

❋   ❋   ❋

As soon as Dad drops me off, I hurry inside. I have English first period, and I take a seat in the middle of the room. I recognize some of the kids from last year but see lots of new faces.

Ms. Lewis says that seventh grade will be much harder than sixth, and we have to take charge of our own education. "You are the ones responsible for putting forth your best effort." Her voice is monotone. I wish I could take my book out of my backpack and read, but I'm in the second row so she would definitely notice. I look out the window toward Fenwick and wonder how Fan is doing on her first day at an American high school.

Second period is world history. Mr. Freeman holds up a big jar that says SUGAR on the outside. "Can anyone guess why I brought this to school?" he asks.

One girl raises her hand. "For your coffee?"

"Good guess," he says. "But I drink it black. Anyone else?"

Nobody has any other ideas.

"Because sugar changed the world." He tells us that you can trace history if you follow a single product. For example, sugar cane was responsible for the rise of the slave trade in the United States, he explains, and for ending slavery in England. I really like the way he jumps right into the class instead of talking about grading and responsibility and school policy. I can tell that world history is going to be great.

"Anna!"

I turn around and Hideat, a girl I know from CAT, is right behind me. She takes my arm and pulls me along to the cafeteria. "I'm so glad we have the same lunch bell." We find seats in the back by the window. "How was your summer?"

"Kind of boring. What about yours?"

"I watched my little sister most of the time." Hideat opens her lunch container and offers me a section of her orange. "Where's Camille?"

"She's going to Springer this year."

"What's that?"

I wonder if I should tell people that Camille is in a special school, but then I remember that she is always so open about everything. "It's a school for kids with learning disabilities."

Hideat looks surprised. "I know she didn't get really good grades, and she always seemed so worried about school, but I didn't know it was that serious."

"Her parents wanted her to go," I say. "Hopefully just for one year." Then I tell Hideat about Fan, how I met her when I was in China, and how she's at the high school as an exchange student for the year.

"Is she living with you?" Hideat asks.

"With Andee." I look out the window and there is Fan, eating lunch with a group of kids on the high school patio. Sam from CAT is sitting next to Fan, and a blond girl is on her other side. But where is Andee?

The bell rings and we hurry to our third class. The rest of the day goes by slowly—art, math, and Spanish. I know a few kids from last year, but none of them is my friend, and I think this is going to be a very long year.

Chapter Seven

The Weekend

$\mathcal{M}$om arranges with Mrs. Wu for Fan to spend the weekend with us. When they get to our house, I ask Andee if she wants to stay over too, but she seems in a hurry to leave. "I already have tons of homework," she says.

"Do you want to plan our first joint CAT meeting? I bet my dad could take you home later."

Andee looks sideways at Fan, who is sitting on the floor with Ken. "I think we'd better wait." She pushes open the screen door.

As I watch Andee cross our yard, I remember how she used to love being at my house with Kaylee and

Ken and commotion all around. She said her house was too quiet, and she wished she had a noisy family like mine. But now she'd rather do her homework in the car. Does she need a break from Fan? Or from me? Kaylee is putting her sock mouse on top of Ken's Lego robot's head. Ken keeps taking it off. Maow Maow is watching from underneath the sofa. "I like your family," Fan says.

I join them on the floor. "Do you like Fenwick High?" I ask.

"The teachers talk very, very fast. I think I cannot study well. But I will try hard every day. I will not . . . give up."

"When I first got to China, I couldn't understand people either. I think it takes a while."

"Yes. Andee's mother says that too. She says join activities and talk to people is the way to learn. So I want to join volleyball." Fan sighs. "Students are very nice. They want to help me."

"That's good," I say.

"Andee does not join anything." Fan looks concerned. "She fights with her mother. Every day they fight."

"About what?"

"I don't understand what they say." She pats Kaylee's head. "I think Andee is not very . . ." She searches for the word. "Like my friend in China. She does not have many friends to talk."

I think about that. In middle school, Andee ate lunch with Sam and a few other kids every day, and she spoke easily at the CAT meetings. She seemed pretty sociable compared to me. What has changed for her in high school?

Kaylee plunks herself on my lap with a Babar book. "Read it to me," she says.

"Not now," I say.

Kaylee pushes out her lower lip and pouts. "Just like my Little Monkey brother," Fan says. "He wants me to play with him. But sometimes I am tired of play."

"You must miss your family." I remember how homesick I felt in China when I looked at photos of Ken and Kaylee.

"Yes, I miss everybody. My mother writes me a letter. She says the big problem is my grandfather is not feeling good. And they must send money for medicine every week." Fan takes out her notebook. "The important thing is I must study very well." She shows me her list of new words: *lawyer, pharmacy, orthodontist, braces, tighten, extended family, nuclear family, debate, popular, sociable.* She asks me to say them and then she repeats after me.

"Your pronunciation is good," I say.

"Not so good," she says. "The students at Fenwick don't understand me very well. And I don't understand them." She sighs. "Especially Andee. She talks not very clear." Fan pauses. "I must listen."

Later, Fan is moving her lips in her sleep and I wonder if she is practicing her new vocabulary words. I remember lying in the hotel room in Beijing and saying new Chinese words and phrases over and over in my head. Sometimes in the morning they were still there, but other times I couldn't remember a thing.

On Saturday morning, Camille is waiting outside the church where we have our Chinese class. As soon as she sees us, she runs over and gives me a hug. "It seems like I haven't seen you in forever."

"I know!" I say. "How's Springer?"

She pushes her bangs out of her eyes. "The teachers are nice, but I miss Fenwick." She turns to Fan. "How do you like American high school?"

"I like to study. But my English is not good."

I introduce Fan to Teacher Zhao. He is glad to have a teacher's helper, and Fan says the words and phrases clearly so we can get the tones right. She also teaches us a new song. At Chinese school, Fan seems more like she did in China, sure and comfortable.

"This song is very popular in China," she says.

"You used one of your new words," I say.

Fan smiles. "Every night I practice."

On the way home, we stop at the library and I show Fan where they have the poetry books. She picks out

Where the Sidewalk Ends and a book with poems by lots of different authors. Then I show her the chapter books novels, and we borrow *Charlotte's Web* and *Superfudge*. Fan says that even though some of the books are for younger kids, they will help her learn English. She looks around the library. "This is my favorite place," she says.

"Mine too," I say. I tell her how in fourth grade, I read so much that my parents were worried.

"Reading is the key for the world. That's what my teacher told me," Fan says. "My little brother doesn't like to read. But I make him so he can grow up smart and help my family." Fan opens the poetry book and starts reading out loud:

"'Soothing Sea Sounds' by Aufie Zophy:
'Soothing, breaking one by one,
Peaceful brushing on the shore
In crescendo and then back down
My soul is asking for much more.'"

Fan reads the poem again silently. "I never see the sea," she says.

"I saw it near Shanghai," I say. "And once we drove to the beach in North Carolina."

She reads the poem a third time. "I cannot understand all the words, but this poem has sound like water."

Chapter Eight

News from China

Fan goes to school with Andee during the week and stays with us most weekends. We have Chinese class on Saturdays, and after that Fan spends most of her time on her homework. She has trouble understanding the textbooks, especially *Ancient and Medieval History*. I try to help, but she reads so slowly that by the time we get to the end of the chapter, she has lost the meaning. I write her a summary of the whole chapter like I used to do for Camille so she can at least get the main idea.

Every time Andee and her mom drop Fan off, I ask Andee to join us, but she never wants to stay.

"Do you want to think about some possible CAT projects?" I ask again.

She shakes her head. "Not yet." I notice that she has had her nose pierced, and she is wearing a tiny diamond stud.

"Why don't you stay and do homework with us?" I ask.

Andee looks so put together in her blue shorts and sleeveless top. Her neck is slender like a model's. But something in her face looks unsettled. She watches Fan go up the stairs. "Does she complain about me?" she whispers.

I shake my head.

"Just wondering." Andee takes a deep breath.

"Okay, I'd better go. See you later."

Andee goes out to the car. I want to run after her and say, *Andee, wait, you used to love it at my house, remember?* But she has already shut the car door. I stand in the doorway, staring out into the front yard. The wind is cool and leaves are blowing off the apple tree. I go back inside to get my sweatshirt, then step outside. Fall has always been my favorite time of year. After months of heat and humidity, I love the smell of leaves and the taste of crisp Jonathan apples. But today I feel like crying. Andee obviously doesn't like Fan, and now it seems as if she doesn't like me either. And Fan is not very happy, especially when she gets low grades. For a moment I wish Fan had never come to America in the first place. Then Andee would have gotten a regular AFS student who had studied English for many years and wore fashionable clothes like hers.

The wind blows my hair across my face. I feel like taking a long walk by myself, but I can't just leave Fan alone in the house. I take a deep breath and go back into the living room.

❄ ❄ ❄

Fan shows me her history quiz. There are ten short-answer questions, and she only got credit for two. "Very terrible," she says.

"That's because English is not your first language," I say.

She closes her eyes. "I must study more." She sits on the edge of my bed and reads the history book, mouthing the words silently.

I look through my planner. I have to answer ten questions about *To Kill a Mockingbird* for English and do a page of math problems, but I don't feel like doing either. The only teacher I really like this year is Mr. Freeman. I love the way he teaches history by focusing on a specific thing. First it was sugar, and now we're looking at salt. I never knew that salt used to be considered something really valuable, almost like gold. In the Middle Ages, people even fought wars over it. Mr. Freeman shows us how we can see the history of the world in something so ordinary, something we use every day.

I open my math book to page 92, but instead of copying the problems into my notebook, I write a note to Andee.

Dear Andee,
I wonder why you seem so different from how you used to be. I am guessing

it has something to do with Fan. Or have
I hurt your feelings? Is something else
wrong?

I start doodling in the corner of the page. I have so
many questions, but I don't think I should interrogate
Andee. Maybe I should try to tell her how I feel instead:

When you went out to sit in the car
today, I felt like crying. I remembered how
you used to love to come over to my
house, and suddenly I wished we had never
invited Fan to come to America, and things
would be like they used to be. But maybe
that's not true because I know things
always change.
Your friend, Anna

After I sign my name, my eyes get teary. I reach for
a tissue and blow my nose.

Fan looks up. "You cannot do the problems?" she asks.

"I'm starting over," I say, flipping the note over quickly and copying the first math problem onto a clean page.

❄ ❄ ❄

After lunch, Fan sits down at the computer and finds a message from home. She is happy at first, but then her face drops. "My grandfather is sick again," she says. She reads the short note several times. Then she sits on the sofa and stares at the cover of the history book.

I sit next to her. "Maybe it's not so serious. Maybe he just has the flu."

"My mother is working in the day and in the night. Baba too. They need to buy medicine for Gong Gong. Now I cannot help."

"Do you want to go back to China?"

Fan raises her eyebrows. "I cannot give up. I cannot disappoint my family."

Mom comes in carrying Kaylee, and I tell her about

the email. She sits on the other side of Fan with Kaylee on her lap. "You are our daughter in America," Mom says in Chinese. "But you have your first family in China. Please ask your mother how we can help."

"*Xie xie,*" Fan says, then opens the history book and starts reading.

Mom takes Andee's mom into the kitchen when she comes to get Fan. I hear them talking in low voices, and I guess Mom is telling her about Fan's grandfather.

Instead of going out to wait in the car, Andee opens her backpack. "Can you help me with my Chinese homework?" she asks Fan.

"Fan's grandfather is sick," I say.

"Is it serious?" Andee asks, sitting next to Fan at the dining room table.

"Sick is serious," Fan says. Then she takes Andee's notebook and corrects the mistakes with her purple pen. "Write the Chinese words like this." Her voice is clear and sure. She shows Andee how to make the strokes in the right order.

Andee tries again.

"No," Fan says. "This way." She takes the pen and rewrites three of the characters.

"Mine look the same," Andee says.

"No," Fan says. "Not the same. Chinese writing must look beautiful. This way. One, two, three, four."

Andee tries once more.

"Better," Fan says.

"Thank you for helping me." Andee is controlling her voice and speaking more slowly than usual. "I'm sorry to hear about your grandfather. I hope he feels better soon."

"He is not better." Fan stands up, crosses the living room, and walks slowly up the stairs.

Andee looks at me. "We can send money to her family," she says. "For medicine or whatever they need. Or, I bet we can get the medicine here if we can find out exactly what it is. My mom uses these international courier services to send things all over the world."

I can tell Andee wants to help, and Fan's grandfather probably does need more medicine, but Andee sounds as if she knows how to solve the problem right away. Shouldn't she first try to understand more about how Fan feels? "I don't think—" I take a deep breath and start again. "When Fan was little, she stayed with her grandparents in the countryside while her parents lived in Beijing to earn more money. Her grandparents really raised her."

"So what do you think they need?"

"We should ask Fan. She's the one who knows."

"I wonder if Fan should go back to China." Andee swallows hard. "I think she's been pretty unhappy with us. Even if she doesn't go back, she should live with you." Her voice breaks. "Maybe she'd be happier." Then Andee is talking and crying at once. "Everything I suggest, she just shakes her head. All she ever wants to do is study. We even asked her if she wanted to see New York City, and she said no." Andee looks up. "We try to be generous, but she— I really think she'd be better off with your family. But of course my parents completely disagree."

I reach for my notebook, tear out the page with my note, and hand it to Andee. Her eyes move quickly over the words.

"Sorry," she says. Her voice comes out in a whisper. "It's really not your fault."

Instantly, I feel better. But there is still so much I don't understand.

Andee takes a deep breath. "Now that her grandfather is sick, maybe she really should go home. I asked her if she wanted to, but she said she doesn't want to disappoint her family."

"She's only been here for two months," I say.

"It feels like forever."

Fan is coming down the stairs. She has washed her face and pulled her hair back into a tight ponytail. I wonder if she heard what Andee said.

Andee's mother comes into the living room and puts her arm around Fan's shoulders. "When we get home, we will talk about next steps," she says.

Fan stands stiffly without answering. Then the three of them walk out to the car.

Chapter Nine

CAT

Hideat and I decide to have the first CAT meeting without the high schoolers. We put flyers up in the middle school halls on Monday, and eleven students show up in Mr. Freeman's room on Wednesday afternoon.

I feel nervous about running the meeting, but once we get started, everything falls into place. There are five sixth-graders, four seventh-graders including Hideat and me, and two eighth-graders. I write an agenda on the board the way Andee always did. Then I show a Power Point presentation of the projects we did last year: mentoring first-graders, fundraising for an orphanage in Africa, and knitting hats for ba-

bies in China. I ask everyone to brainstorm about things they would like to do this year. One girl says we could organize a book drive for Children's Hospital. A boy says we could volunteer as tutors for the Literacy Alliance to help people learn to read. Hideat takes notes on everything, and we agree to try to find out more about the specific organizations that we could help and to meet again next week.

"You kids have quite a thing going," Mr. Freeman says after the other students are gone. He wants to know more about the activities we did last year, so I tell him about my trip to Kaylee's orphanage in China to deliver the hats. He listens hard. "You kids really do things," he says. "Not just talk about them." He smiles. "I guess that makes sense, Community *Action* Team. Keep me in the loop if I can help."

Talking to Mr. Freeman makes me miss the old Andee. Last year, she was the one who was always ready to make a plan of action, not me. She was the one with the notebook full of steps to take.

I glance at the clock. It's three thirty, and Dad is coming to pick me up in an hour. Fan said she has volleyball practice after school on Wednesdays, so I head over to the gym. I take a shortcut across the field between the middle school and the high school. The air is warm, but the wind is strong. It blows dust from the field into a cloud that stings my eyes. I hurry toward the school building.

When I get to the gym, Fan is in the back row, holding the ball. She plants her feet, tosses the ball, and slams it over the net. The other team can't return her power serve.

"Way to go!" the coach calls.

A couple of the girls pat Fan on the back.

Instead of doing my homework, I sit in the bleachers and watch the practice. Fan is the shortest one on the team, but she jumps higher than everyone else and slams the ball down fast. She seems confident and sure on the court, like she did on the crowded bus in China. But most of the rest of the time in America, like at my house or at Andee's, at the grocery store, or in the school hallway, she seems small and scared.

The girls on the volleyball team look like adults to me, and suddenly I feel self-conscious in my baggy T-shirt with my flat chest. When I told Mom I wanted to get a bra, she said Asians usually mature later, and I really don't need one yet.

When the game is over, the girls cluster around Fan. The coach has a big flip chart showing all the schools they are going to play against, and the tournament dates. "I'll send everyone an email with the schedule," she says. "Make sure you come to every practice. And don't forget to do your exercises at home."

Fan sees me and walks over to the bleachers. "Hi, Anna. You stay after school today?"

"I had the Community Action Team meeting."

The coach comes by and tells Fan that she should run laps to keep up her endurance. I'm not sure if Fan understands, but she nods.

"You're really good," I say.

Fan looks over at the coach and lowers her voice. "I like volleyball. But I have to stop. I have to study. Volleyball has no future, but study English can help my family." Fan picks up her jacket.

"I don't think you should quit," I say. "You're the best one on the team."

Fan shakes her head. "Study more is better."

I remember what Andee said about how Fan never wants to do anything except study. Maybe she really is stubborn. We go outside and stand by the curb. The wind is gusty now, and leaves are swirling off the maple tree. One lands in the hood of Fan's sweatshirt. "That's good luck," I say.

Fan doesn't understand.

"If you catch a leaf, you will have good luck."

"The leaf catches me is still good luck?" Fan asks.

"Yes! Maybe that means you will win the volleyball tournament."

Fan takes the leaf out of her hood. "The meaning is Gong Gong will get well," she says.

Soon after I get home the phone rings, and I am surprised to hear Andee's voice. "Fan said you had a CAT meeting."

"We met after school in Mr. Freeman's room."

"I thought we were going to do CAT together," she says.

"But you said you were too busy."

"I just said I didn't want to start right away." Andee's voice has an edge that I've never heard before.

Kaylee is chasing Ken around the kitchen while Dad is cooking dinner. Andee is right. I should have asked her again before I just scheduled a meeting. I want to tell Andee that I'm sorry, and that we can schedule the next meeting together. I want to see if she can come over so we can plan some projects. I want to ask her what high school is really like. But I can hardly talk.

"Did you schedule the next meeting?" she asks.

My voice comes out in a whisper. "It's after Thanksgiving. On Wednesday."

"Okay."

Andee doesn't say "See you soon" or anything like that. All she says is "Bye."

Chapter Ten
The Swallow

Andee's family is going skiing in Vermont over Thanksgiving. They invite Fan, but she doesn't want to go. Andee and her mother bring her over on Tuesday night, and she goes right upstairs to study.

"I told you," Andee says.

"I think she's really worried about her grandfather."

"We've told her that she can call anytime she wants, and that we'll buy her a ticket home if she decides to go. We even offered to buy her another ticket to come back again if she wants to finish the school year. We've suggested just about everything we can think of."

Andee's voice is getting louder, and I feel the usual

lump growing in my throat, but this time I will not let it keep me from talking. "Fan thinks that studying is the only way she can help her family."

Andee cuts me off. "Don't you think I know that? You think I know nothing about different cultures when I've traveled all over the place ever since I was born? Fan is the one who is closed-minded."

The late-afternoon sun is coming through the window and reflecting the blue stone in Andee's necklace. Her face looks beautiful with her long neck and frizzy hair. But her eyes are angry. "Why would she come to another country if she just wants to hole up in a room?" she adds.

My voice is louder. "You can't tell her what she should do. You don't know what she feels like or anything about her life."

"I ask her about her life all the time. But there's nothing I can do if she won't talk. At least not to me."

Andee's cheeks are red and her eyes are swollen and I suddenly feel sorry for her. Then we see that Fan has been standing in the hallway, listening. She has on her pajamas like the first night she arrived, and her hair is a mess. "I'm sorry," she says. *"Dui bu qui."* She gives me a piece of paper and runs back upstairs.

I read the note silently and hand it to Andee:

One girl,
two sad eyes.
Thanksgiving is coming
and I give thanks
to two girls,
my sisters in America.
I am sorry.

Andee's mom comes into the living room. "We better get going. We have to pack up all of our skiing things tonight, and our plane leaves at six in the morning." She doesn't seem to notice her daughter's red cheeks and watery eyes.

"Have a good time," Mom says. "And be careful on the mountain."

Andee opens the door, and a blast of cold air hits my face.

"I think winter's coming early," her mom says. She grabs Andee's arm and they hurry to their car.

When I go upstairs, Fan is lying on the very edge of my bed, sound asleep. I get my pajamas on in the dark and slip into bed.

In the middle of the night, I hear a sound. Is it the wind? Or Ken coming in to spend the night? Then I feel the bed move and I see that it is Fan, trying to muffle her sobs in her pillow.

"What's wrong?" I whisper.

She doesn't answer.

"Are you worried about your grandfather?"

She looks at me in the near dark. "Everything. Grandfather and Mama and Baba and Little Monkey." She wipes her nose on her sleeve. "And you and Andee."

"Me?"

She takes a deep breath. "Andee is your friend. When you were in China, she makes you good-luck fortunes. And now you fight. It is my fault."

"It's our fault," I say.

"Andee is not happy with me," Fan says.

"Maybe you should do more things with her family," I say. "I think it will be fun."

Fan sits up. "I come to America for success. Not for fun."

"I know. But . . ." I don't know how to explain myself in English or in Chinese. "I think you should try."

"I am trying," Fan says. "Every day I study so many new words."

"I mean try to join Andee and her family," I say.

"Andee does not listen when I talk."

"Maybe you don't listen to her, either."

Fan lies back down and turns onto her stomach with her face in the pillow.

"Fan?"

She doesn't answer.

I turn toward the window. Soon Andee will be on a ski slope in Vermont. I wish I could talk to her right now. Fan really is stubborn. She wants to do things the way she did in China, the way she was taught, and when you suggest a new way, she shuts down. Andee has her ideas too. I guess everyone is like that because the only person's life you really know is your own.

In the morning, Fan has an email message saying that her grandfather is better. He is eating more now and gaining strength. Her mother says Fan shouldn't worry, just study. But Fan still looks upset.

"Mama is not telling me truth," Fan says.

"How do you know?"

"I know," Fan says. But when I ask her how she knows, she just shakes her head. Then she shows me that she got her first A in English on the poetry unit. "I like it," she says, showing me a Chinese poem about a swallow, which she translated and then analyzed for her es-say. She tells me how when she was little and she was stay-ing in the countryside with her grandparents, she used

to cry at night because she missed her mom. "Grandmother Po Po sings me this swallow song."

I read the words:

> A little swallow
> wears beautiful feathers.
> Every spring
> it will come back.
> I ask the swallow,
> Why do you come here?
> Spring is the most beautiful
> at home,
> the swallow says.

Fan hands me her essay.

> Migrants in China are like the swallow. Every spring, if they can save enough money, they go home for the spring festival (Chinese New Year). When I was in Beijing with my parents, we try to go home to the countryside like the swallow in spring. Sometimes we go, but sometimes we don't

have enough money for so many train tickets. Then we get the train tickets with no seat and I sleep standing against Baba's legs. The train is so crowded like matches in a box. Everybody standing up tall to reach the air. I am small and hard to breathe. But I don't complain because Grandmother Po Po and Grandfather Gong Gong wait for me. In my head, I sing the swallow song.

When we get to the station is very muddy in spring because much rain. Mama scolds me if I step in the puddle. But then I see Grandmother Po Po and Grandfather Gong Gong and I know a train ride and mud are not important. Gong Gong smiles so beautiful and I know I come home.

Fan says she wrote her essay in Chinese first and then translated it into English. "Andee's mother says it's better to write in English first, but then I lose the meaning," Fan says. "First Chinese, then I translate."

"Maybe you should try writing directly in English," I say. "I think it will be a lot faster."

"No," Fan says, with that stubborn look on her face that I've seen often lately.

I reread the swallow poem. "Are you still homesick?"

Fan nods. "My whole life I am homesick. In Beijing I am homesick because I miss the countryside. In the countryside, I am homesick because I miss friends in Beijing. And in America, I am homesick for my family."

"Why didn't your grandparents go with you to Beijing?" I ask.

Fan shakes her head. "Grandfather Gong Gong and Grandmother Po Po are farmers. They are not happy in a big city."

"How old were you when you left the countryside to live with your parents?"

"Eight," she says.

"Maybe you should tell Andee more about your life," I say.

"She is not patient," Fan says.

"If she was patient, you would not be in America."

※　※　※

Fan sits on the sofa with the history book the entire afternoon. I sit in the armchair and read *The Diary of Anne Frank*. It's funny how her situation and mine have nothing in common, but still I feel a lot like Anne. She writes about feeling irritated at people in the small attic hideout, especially her mom, often for no real reason. Lately I've been feeling like that too. Yesterday Mom asked me to wash Kaylee's face and take her out of her highchair, and I rolled my eyes.

I like the way *The Diary of Anne Frank* is written, but there is so much she leaves out. How do people know who is Jewish and who isn't? I look up and see my reflection in the window. Of course everyone knows I am Asian right away. It's the first thing they notice. In some ways, that's easier than if part of who you are is hidden. I wonder how Andee feels. People notice right away that's she's not white, but they have no idea what she is.

I look over at Fan. She has a wide forehead and thick eyebrows. I wonder if in China, people can tell she's a migrant. And if they can tell, do they treat her differently, like at the hotel where she works? I know that migrants are not legal in the cities. That's why they're not allowed to go to the public schools. I wonder if everywhere they go, they feel like they should hide who they are. Is that even possible? Can people tell just by looking at their faces that they are poor farmers who don't belong? I want to talk to Fan about what it's really like to be a migrant in Beijing, but she is trying to study.

Chapter Eleven
Thanksgiving

Thanksgiving is my favorite holiday of the year. I love dinner at Auntie Linda's and playing old games like Twister in Camille's basement with all the other Chinese families. Plus, this year, Grandma is here from California and is staying until Christmas!

"She's going to help me make a Lego helicopter," Ken says.

"Me too," Kaylee says.

Ken glares at Kaylee. "She didn't say that."

Usually Grandma and I do a sewing project together. Last year, we sewed a dress for Kaylee. I wonder what we should make this year. A girl in my class has a shirt

I really like that ties in the back, but I think it would be too complicated to make.

Ken wants to make a beanbag toss game, so he and Dad go to get the plywood. Grandma and I decide to sew the beanbags out of fabric scraps. We use the sewing machine to make square pockets, which we fill with kidney beans. The whole time we are sewing, Fan is sitting on the sofa with the ancient and medieval history book, reading the chapter out loud. There are many words she pronounces wrong, like "Graeco-Roman," "Phoenicians," and "disarray," and I wonder if she knows their meanings. Suddenly she looks up. "I think this book is wrong."

"What do you mean?"

"This book is ancient history. But only one chapter about China. I think China has a long ancient history." Fan shows me with her hands.

"Maybe you should ask the teacher about that."

She looks surprised. "How can I ask the teacher? I am a student."

"I think you should ask the teacher why there is so little about China."

Fan looks at me like I'm crazy and turns back to her textbook.

The weather has turned warmer again, and when we go to Camille's house for Thanksgiving dinner, everyone is outside. We set the game up in the backyard, divide into teams, and start tossing the beanbags into the holes. I ask Fan if she wants to play, but she shakes her head. Instead she sits on the porch steps with the textbook open on her lap. Auntie Linda sits down next to Fan and talks to her a mile a minute in Chinese. I don't know exactly what she's saying, but it's something about too much studying. She sets the book on the porch table and tells Fan not to pick it up until it's time to go home.

I remember when I was younger, we were all together for Thanksgiving and I wanted to read instead of playing with the other kids. Auntie Linda took my book and set it by the front door. At first I was mad and embarrassed, but then I found that playing Twister was actually really fun. It occurs to me suddenly that Fan might be studying to avoid doing something else. But what? Is she afraid of talking in English? Or could it be that she is she afraid to make friends in America?

The neighbor's dog keeps trying to catch the beanbags. Finally he intercepts my toss and carries the beanbag away underneath their porch. The only one small enough to get it is  Kaylee. She comes out with the beanbag in her mouth like the dog, and Fan, Camille, Ken, and I laugh until our stomachs ache.

After dinner, Fan says that she used to play a game in China with small bags filled with rice. We sit in Camille's basement and sew the little pouches. When we're done, Fan shows us how to play. You have to try to pick up the small rice bags one at a time until you have them all, kind of like jacks. Camille has big hands, but she is clumsy and the bags keep dropping. We end up tossing the bags to each other like in a game of hot potato.

When it's time to go home, Fan says this is the most fun she's had since she's been in America. "I don't think about study or Gong Gong or anything." She buckles her seatbelt. "I feel used to America now—a little."

"I think it takes time to get used to things."

Fan nods. "Sometimes I worry too much."

"About what?"

Fan is concentrating hard to answer. "When I speak English, I feel different, not like a Chinese girl."

I think about that for a few seconds. "Camille speaks English and Chinese, and she seems like . . . that's just part of who she is."

Fan nods. "You are right. Two languages is better." Then, as we're pulling out of the driveway, she says, "When Andee comes back, we can teach her the rice bag game."

※　※　※

Friday we take Fan to her final volleyball tournament against two other high schools. Fenwick wins the first game but loses the second. There is a girl on Central's team who serves just as hard as Fan, and the Fenwick girls have trouble returning her balls. Fenwick ends up taking second place. The coach congratulates everybody and says they had a good season. "We hope all of you sophomores and juniors come back and play with us again."

"I cannot play volleyball next year," Fan says to me.

"Maybe you can find a team in China."

"No," Fan says. "Next year I will work at the hotel."

On Saturday a card arrives in the mail from Andee. On the front she has pasted a snowflake. I open the note:

> Dear Anna,
> In this snowy place, I have time to think about

things. I miss you and Fan. I hope you are having a nice Thanksgiving break.

    Love,

    Andee

Underneath she drew her face with a ski cap and curly hair sticking out. All around her are snowflakes.

The picture reminds me of all the paper fortune cookies Andee made for me when I went to China, with their tiny drawings and short messages. I loved opening them at night in our hotel room and feeling connected to home. Andee writes that being in the snowy mountains gives her time to think, but I wish I knew what she has been thinking.

Over break, I finish *Anne Frank*. We studied the Holocaust in fifth grade, and I've already read *Number the Stars,* but this book is much sadder to me because the diary is real. Eight months after Anne Frank wrote the last entry, she and her sister died. I look at her face on the cover, with her dark eyes and slight smile. Despite everything that was happening, Anne was cheerful and hopeful most of the time.

I ask Fan if she wants to go with me to the library, but she wants to study as usual, so I go by myself. The sun is shining though the air is cool. I zip my sweatshirt and pull up the hood. The leaves on the ground rustle as I walk. In fourth grade, Camille and Laura and I used to bury ourselves in big piles of leaves and gather buckeyes in our pockets. I wish they were walking with me now.

When I get to the library, I browse around all the new kids' books, but nothing looks interesting. What do I really feel like reading?

There is a photography exhibit in the display case called "Children Around the World." One is of a boy looking very worried, with no shirt on, squinting into the sun. *New York City,* it says. Another is of an Asian girl peeling potatoes with her grandfather at a table outside in Ho Chi Minh City. I look at all the pictures, wondering if there might be one of migrant kids in China, but there isn't. Then I ask the librarian if they have any books about Chinese migrants. "Do you mean immigrants?" she asks. I shake my head. "I mean migrants inside China." She looks it up on the computer and there are two, she says, in the stacks. I sit down at the table to wait.

One book, called *From Somewhere to Nowhere,* is full of photographs. On the cover it has a picture of a woman with a kerchief on her head, looking down and away from the camera. First I think she is Mom's age, but then I see that she is actually much younger, maybe even a teenager. The other book, *Factory Girls,* is about two teenage girls who left their homes in the countryside to work in factories in the city. I check the books out, put them in my backpack, and head home.

Before we go to bed, Fan and I look at the photo book together. Fan is quiet, staring at each picture for a minute before turning the page. There is one of a baby squatting on the ground while his mother pushes coal in a wheelbarrow. Another shows young women on an assembly line. Fan stops at a picture of a man shoveling rubble into a cart. "Like my Baba," she says. Then she turns to me. "The pictures in the book are sad. But migrants are not always sad." She shows me another picture of a family headed home for Spring Festival. The man is carrying lots of packages and he has a wide smile on his face as he hurries toward his relatives. "Sometimes sad and sometimes happy," Fan says. "Like me, too."

"Are you sad at Andee's house?"

Fan thinks before replying. "I will try more." She closes the book. "Are you sad or happy?"

"I'm lonely at school without Camille," I say. "And without Andee. But I like Hideat and I like Mr. Freeman's class."

Fan nods. "Without friends is sad." She moves her hand over the cover of the book. "Thank you for this book about migrants in China. It makes me remember." Fan hesitates. "In Beijing I am not a Beijing person. I am always a migrant."

"Do you wish you were a Beijing person?"

Fan looks frustrated by my question. "I can never be

a Beijing person. I do not talk like a Beijing person and I do not look like a Beijing person." She looks down. "America it is different."

"What do you mean?"

"In America, they don't know what is a migrant. They only know Chinese. But if I have this book, I can explain my life."

On Sunday, Fan gets an email from her mother. She says Little Monkey did well on his first report card so they are proud of him. Fan smiles. "I know my brother is so smart," she says. "But he is also lazy."

We spend the afternoon making more rice bags out of scraps. Fan wants to make a set for Andee. "She likes this material?" Fan asks, pointing to blue fabric with yellow dots. "Or this?" She holds up black material with small orange candy corn all over it.

"The yellow dots," I say, remembering that Andee loved a polka-dotted dress I once made for Kaylee.

Before bed, Fan goes down to check her email since it is morning in China. I sit at my desk and make a card for Andee. On the front, I glue snippets of fabric. Inside I write:

> Dear Andee,
> Thank you for the card. The little drawing reminds me of last year and all the fun we had together. I wonder what you have been thinking.
> Love, Anna

On Sunday evening, Andee and her mom come to get Fan. "The snow was great this year," Andee's mom says. "And I finally got off the bunny slope." She explains to Fan that the bunny slope is for beginners.

"I thought you can ski very well," Fan says.

Andee's mom shakes her head. "Not at all. Little by little, I am making some progress. I grew up in Alabama, and there's no snow there."

Andee's mom and my mom go into the kitchen to have a cup of tea, and for the first time in a while,

Andee doesn't seem in a hurry to leave. Fan gives her the rice bags and we show her how to play. Kaylee keeps coming and saying she wants to play too, but of course she can't catch the rice bags. We end up juggling them, which she thinks is really funny. Maow Maow watches from the corner and pounces each time we drop a bag.

Before they leave, I give Andee the card. She runs her fingers over the fabric, unfolds the paper, and lets her eyes move over the words. "Thanks," she says. "I love the way you arranged the fabric scraps." She folds the card carefully and puts it into her pocket.

Fan asks if she can borrow the photo book. "I want to show Andee," she says.

Later that evening, I start reading the book about the factory girls. The beginning is about a teenager who leaves her home in the countryside to join her sister, who is working in an electronics factory. She works on an assembly line for thirteen hours each day and sleeps in a factory dormitory with eleven other factory girls. They become good friends, but they also fight a lot. Then, when one of them leaves to work in a different factory, everyone forgets about her. I cannot imagine sleeping in a crowded stuffy room, and then waking up to work for so many hours assembling parts of alarm clocks, calculators, phones, and computers. I glance at the clock on my shelf. I wonder if it was made in China. I want to talk to Mr. Freeman about this book.

Just as I'm about to go to bed, the phone rings. "Do you want to stay after school tomorrow?" Andee asks. "To plan some CAT projects?"

Chapter Twelve

The Spring Bud School

$\mathcal{M}$r. Freeman is straightening out his desk. "Hello, Anna. Do you have a CAT meeting today?"

"It's not really a meeting. Just Andee and me. We're trying to do some planning."

"I remember her from last year," he says. "The dynamic duo. I have a meeting at the high school, so I'll leave you to your work."

Andee tosses her backpack onto the floor and joins me at the back table. "All through geometry, I couldn't stop thinking about migrants in China. The whole thing seems so unfair. Fan was telling me that if you don't have an identity card from the city, you're basically illegal."

I don't think I have ever heard Andee say *Fan was telling me* before. I nod. "I think it's like people here who come across the border from Mexico without a visa."

"Except the Chinese migrants don't come from a different country. Fan and I spent a long time looking through all the pictures in the book. There's so much I never knew."

I imagine Andee and Fan sitting next to each other on the bed with the book open between them.

"Fan told me migrants feel like everyone else is better than they are," Andee says.

"It's so unfair. I think people should be able to live wherever they want."

"That's exactly what I told Fan," Andee says. "But she said that in China, the cities are too crowded. They have to try to limit the number of people somehow."

"Do you think Fan wishes she weren't a migrant girl?"

Andee looks out the window. "Fan usually doesn't

think about what she wishes. She accepts things the way they are."

I reach for the CAT notebook in my backpack. "Do you think we could do something to help migrants in China?"

Andee takes a piece of paper out of a folder. "Last night I asked Fan to list the problems of migrant kids." Andee hands me the notebook. In Fan's handwriting it says:

> No hukou (identity card)
> Cannot use public school
> Migrant schools are bad
> Not enough money
> Homesick
> Funny accent in Chinese
> People stare at migrants in the street

"People look at us all the time here too," I say.

Andee nods. "In some ways it's similar but in some ways it's not. When people look at us, they might think we look different, but they don't usually think we're stupid."

"Is that what Chinese think of migrants?"

"That's what Fan said." Andee folds up the paper. "Now I see why she feels she has to study all the time. But I told her that she can learn more if she studies less."

"Did she agree?"

"I don't think so. But she listened." Andee stands up. "There must be something we can do to help migrants. Maybe we can brainstorm at the next meeting." Andee puts her backpack on her shoulder. "I better go. My mom's coming at three thirty." She walks to the door. "It feels strange to be back in middle school. Sometimes I wish I was still here."

"I wish you were, too," I say as we go into the hallway together.

❄ ❄ ❄

Dad is late to pick me up. I wait by the flagpole, watching cars coming around the circle as parents pick up their kids. Even though my backpack is heavy and I have lots of homework, I feel lighter than I have in a long time. Fan and Andee are actually talking to each other!

Just before winter break, we have a surprise snowstorm and school is canceled. Andee's mother drives an SUV with four-wheel drive, so after lunch she brings Fan and Andee over to my house.

Fan checks her email and her mother writes that her brother's school was torn down. The academic level at that school was very low, she explains, so when she heard from one of her friends about a new migrant school in Changping, she decided to send Little Monkey there. He lives in a dormitory at the school during the week and comes home on weekends. The name of the school is Spring Bud Middle School.

Andee, Fan, and I look at the Dandelion website.

The school is in an old factory building like most migrant schools, but inside the walls are painted with colorful murals. Some are made out of bits of colored glass. The text explains that the art teacher and her students collected broken pottery and bottles for over a year, sorted them by color, and then created the mosaic designs. Andee zooms in on a mural of a big yellow flower growing out of a green pot.

"I never see a school like this," Fan says. We spend the afternoon reading everything we can find online about Spring Bud Middle School. It turns out they have volunteers who come to help from American colleges, and some of them have written blogs about their experiences. One girl says, "Spring Bud Middle School changed my life. Now I want to be a teacher or maybe a school principal someday."

"I wonder if they'd like CAT volunteers," I say.

"I wonder if they like a Chinese migrant girl volunteer," Fan says.

Chapter Thirteen

Holiday Break

Andee's family invites Fan to go to Florida with them over the holiday break. They want to show Fan Disney World and Miami Beach. On the way back, they plan to stop to visit Andee's grandparents in Alabama.

"I will stay with you," Fan says.

"Andee's family wants to take you," I say.

"I have to prepare for third quarter," Fan says. She takes the history book out of her backpack. "Eight chapters." She shows me the table of contents. "More than half of the book."

"If you don't go, you will hurt Andee's feelings."

Fan looks down. "Okay, I will go," she says. Then she sits on the sofa reading her book and won't talk to me for the rest of the afternoon.

On the first day of the holiday break, Camille comes with me to babysit for Jing. Even though it's cold out, we take her to the park. She wants to sit in the big-kid swings. "You're too small," I tell her.

She sticks her lower lip out like she is about to cry, then changes her mind when she sees another kid her size in the baby swing.

Camille gives her a push. "I can't believe that I'm a little more than halfway through my year at Springer."

"Are you still counting the days until you can go back to Fenwick?"

Camille nods. "I really miss it."

"But are you glad you're at Springer for now?"

Camille pulls her hat down over her ears. "It's nice not to be the only kid in the class with a learning disability. But I can't say I'm glad to be there."

"Are your stomachaches gone?"

"Better," she says. "But who knows—they might have gotten better anyway." She pushes Jing again. "Do you like seventh grade?"

"It's okay." Jing wants to get out of the swing, so I take her out and set her on the ground. "But I don't have any good friends at school."

"Neither do I," Camille says. "There's a girl named Julie who's nice. But she's really different from me. At least you have Hideat and the other CAT kids."

Camille is right. I am lucky to eat lunch with Hideat every day, and over time, I'm getting to know her better. And lately two other CAT kids have been joining us.

On Christmas Eve, snow flurries are blowing around. Ken and I are hoping for a white Christmas, but so far the snow isn't sticking. Mom invites Camille's family and Ken's friend Alan's family to have dinner with us. She fixes a big roast chicken that I love, and rice and vegetables, and Grandma and I bake an apple cake for dessert.

On Christmas morning, we open our presents.

Grandma gives me green fabric with small yellow swirls and a pattern for exactly the kind of shirt I want. Even though the directions are complicated, she is sure that we can figure it out. We lay the pieces carefully out on the fabric. Kaylee wants to help, but she keeps pulling the fabric off the edge of the table.

"Stop," I say.

She gets mad and throws the whole box of pins.

"No," I say firmly, grabbing her wrist.

She starts crying as if it's my fault that there are pins all over the floor. I feel myself get madder at my sister than I ever have. I know she threw the pins on purpose, and now she's crying and blaming me.

Grandma takes Kaylee out of the room and I start picking the pins up off the floor. Suddenly I wish I had gone to Florida with Andee and Fan. It would be great to sit on the beach in the sun without my pesky sister, and walk along the shore collecting seashells.

I wonder if Fan and Andee are having fun together. They can both laugh a lot, but then they can both be stubborn and sullen. I know that Fan took all her textbooks so she could study. What if she insists on staying in the hotel room reading ancient and medieval history while Andee is alone on the beach?

Kaylee comes back into the room and plunks herself down in the beanbag chair while Grandma and I cut out all the pattern pieces. We're almost done when the phone rings.

"This is Fan," says the voice on the other end. My stomach flips over. Maybe something happened and Fan wants to come home. "I have a question," she continues. "Do you like a bracelet better or a necklace better?"

"A bracelet," I say.

"Do you like snail shell or clam shell?"

"Snail."

"Okay," she says.

I hear laughing in the background, and she hands the phone to Andee. "We had an argument," Andee says. "I said you'd like a clam shell bracelet, and Fan said you'd like a snail shell necklace."

"You're both fifty percent right," I say.

Laura stops over with a plate of cookies for us. Her hair is blonder than it used to be, and she is taller and thin-

ner. But her smile is the same and I realize how much I've missed her.

"Where's your exchange student?" she asks.

"Actually, she's only with us on weekends. She stays with Andee most of the time." I take a cookie. "They took her to Florida this week."

I show Laura the shirt I'm sewing. "I love these kinds of tops that tie in the back," she says, picking up a fabric scrap from the floor. "Remember our drawstring bags? I still use mine."

"Really?" I'm surprised, because I have no idea what happened to mine.

She nods. "I take my lunch to school in it. And now our ecology club is selling them to avoid using so many plastic bags." She smiles. "And each time I take my sandwich out of the bag, I think of you."

"Sometimes I wish we were still at Pleasant Hill," I say. "With Ms. Sylvester."

"I loved Ms. Sylvester and all the stuff you and I did together. But it wasn't a very easy year, with my parents and everything." She pulls her hair back, then lets it go. "Thank goodness that's all over." For a second Laura has the same expression she had in fourth grade, kind of scared and unsure. Then she smiles. "Did I tell you, I'll probably be going to Fenwick High in ninth grade?"

"Really?" Most kids from Our Lady of Angels go on to one of the Catholic high schools.

"My mom only planned to send me to OLA for middle school."

"Would you be glad to come back to public school?"

Laura considers. "I'll miss my friends. But it really is too expensive, and Fenwick is closer." She smiles. "Plus, you're there."

"We could take the bus together," I say.

"Or walk when the weather's good."

Chapter Fourteen

Sad News

Fan had a good time with Andee and her family, and when I see the pictures of the two of them exploring a tide pool, I wish I had been there too.

"What was your favorite part?" I ask Fan.

She thinks for a minute. "The best thing is now I can understand Andee's fast talking most of the time. Oh, and also this." She reaches into her pocket and gives me a bracelet made out of tiny snail shells.

I slip it easily over my hand. "It's perfect!"

Fan smiles. "We made three. One for each. So we can match."

"I wish I had gone with you," I say.

"But there is one bad part. I did not finish all the chapters in the history book." Fan looks really worried.

"You can read some more tonight. If you want, I'll help you with the words you don't know."

I show Fan the blouse Grandma and I made.

"Try it," she says, and I don't feel strange taking my shirt off and slipping on the new one right in front of her. She ties the bow in back for me. "Very nice." She looks at me in the mirror. "Now you look grown up."

After dinner, Fan sits with the history book. "Two more chapters left." She sighs. "Andee showed me how to skim when I read," Fan says. "I think this is like cheating, but Andee says it's fine."

I should be reading *The Incredible Journey* for English class, but I already read it once, and I really don't like Ms. Lewis, so I never feel like doing her assignments. I take out my planner. We have a big project second semester for history. Mr. Freeman wants us to apply what we've learned by researching the history of a specific thing, but I don't know what to pick. I thought about silk or honey, but those are all things we've already talked about in class. I pick up the *Factory Girls* book and thumb through the pages. The migrant teenagers work in factories that make electronics, or clothes and shoes. Suddenly I know. I'll research sneakers.

Fan stands up. "Andee says when I can't pay attention, it's better to take a break." She stretches, goes over to the computer, and logs onto her email account.

I write **Where Sneakers Come From** at the top of my paper, but then I hear Fan suck in her breath. She has her hand over her mouth. I go over to her. She points to the message on the computer screen, but it is in Chinese. The only character that I recognize right away is Gong Gong, *Grandfather*.

Fan turns to face me and her eyes are full of tears. "I was on the beach. That time my grandpa died." She runs up the stairs to my room and shuts the door.

What should I do? Mom and Dad are at work. Ken

is at Alan's. Grandma and Kaylee are in the kitchen. In some ways Fan is very private, but still I cannot leave her alone.

I stand outside the door of my room and knock. There is no answer. I peek in. Fan is sitting at my desk, writing furiously on a legal pad. She doesn't turn toward me and I don't know if she wants me to stay or to leave. Should I put my arm around her? But Fan is not the kind of person who hugs people a lot. "I'm sorry," I whisper. Then I sit on the edge of my bed and pretend to read. Suddenly I really want to talk to Andee, and I tiptoe out of the room.

"Fan's grandfather died," I whisper into the phone.
  "What?"
  "She just got the news."
  "Did she call her mom?"
  "She just ran up to my room and shut the door."
  "Is she crying?"
  "She's sitting at my desk, writing."
  "A letter?"

"I'm not sure."

Andee says that as soon as her mom gets home, they'll be over.

I go back to my room and stand by the bed, staring out the front window. I never met my grandfathers, but I cannot imagine life without Grandma. Whenever we need something, she's the first person we ask, even though she lives so far away. When Kaylee wouldn't eat, Grandma came all the way to Cincinnati to help us.

Fan writes for a long time, tearing off pages as she fills them with small Chinese characters. She stops sometimes to shake out her hand. Finally she puts down the pen and turns to me. "Gong Gong was just like sleeping." Tears are running down her cheeks, but she is speaking clearly in English. "I didn't say good-bye." She swallows hard. "But Gong Gong knows. I am like the swallow. I will go home."

"Do you want to go home now?" I whisper. "We can change your ticket. Maybe you should call your mom and talk to her."

"Gong Gong is already gone," Fan says.

"But if you want to be with your family, you can go."

I hear the front door open—Mom is home. I hurry downstairs to tell her the news.

Andee and her mother are at our house in twenty minutes. "We can get Fan a ticket for tomorrow or the day after," Mrs. Wu says.

"I'm not sure," Mom says.

"What do people in China usually do when their relatives die?"

Mom considers. "Each family is different."

"I think Fan should stay here with you tonight," Andee says. Her face looks scared, like it did the day Fan arrived. "I don't know what to say to her."

Then we see Fan coming down the stairs, clutching the legal pad against her sweater.

"I'm so sorry," Andee's mom says.

Andee and I walk up to meet Fan, and we stand together on the landing. "What would help?" Andee whispers.

"I must make a fire," Fan asks.

"In the fireplace?" I ask.

"Outside." Fan goes to the closet to get her jacket, and Ken, Andee, and I follow her out to the backyard.

"I know where there are lots of sticks," Ken says, going underneath the honeysuckle bushes behind the garage. Soon we have a whole pile of twigs. Ken gets some newspaper and rolls it into logs on the bottom of the grill, and we put the twigs on top. Mom gives me a box of matches and watches us through the back door.

"Do you want to light it?" I ask Fan.

She strikes a match and holds it to the edge of the newspaper. The orange flame sputters for a minute, then catches. Soon the twigs are burning. Then Fan takes the pages she has written and lays them on top.

We stand together around the fire, watching the flames burn first the edges of the yellow paper and then move quickly across until there is nothing left but ashes. I am in the middle between Andee and Fan. Ken is on the other side. As the fire burns down, we move closer, trying to catch the warmth.

When finally there is only smoke, we follow Fan into the house. "Do you want to spend the night?" I ask Andee.

Andee does not answer right away. "Do you want me to?"

I nod.

Fan is sitting on the edge of my bed, still wearing her coat. Andee is standing in the doorway. "Should we get our pajamas on?" I ask.

Fan's eyes look far away. "I am a lucky girl," she says. "Gong Gong lives a long time. When I was a baby, my mother says I cried a lot. Gong Gong carried me all day. That is the only way I can stop crying. When I was bigger, he played little games with me, like hiding a walnut in one hand, and I guess which hand. When I find the walnut, he cracks it open for me so I can eat the inside." Fan stands up. "Gong Gong likes to know everything. Whenever I see him, he says, 'Fan Fan, tell me about your life in the city.' And I tell him about the hotel and Little Monkey. He is never tired because he wants to know." She takes a deep breath. "In my letter, I wrote everything to Gong Gong, so when we burn it, he will know about Florida and Disney World. He will know about Fenwick High School and volleyball and both of you and Ken and Kaylee. He will know about America."

"Do you want to go home?" I ask.

"Tomorrow I can call Mama," she says, closing her eyes. "Gong Gong is her father. Mama will know what to do."

Chapter Fifteen

A Decision

Fan talks to her mother on the phone for a long time, and they decide that she should not return to China now. Her mother says that there is nothing to do, that Uncle and Auntie are looking after Po Po, and that Gong Gong would not like it if everybody disrupted everything for him. Her mother says they are planning to return to the countryside for Spring Festival if they can save enough money for the tickets. Maybe Fan can come back then and they can all go together.

Andee, Fan, and I look at the calendar Fan gave us when she arrived. This year Spring Festival, which

Americans call Chinese New Year, is in the middle of February. That means Fan has less than two more months in the United States.

"Not very long," Fan says. "When I go home, I cannot see Gong Gong." Her eyes get teary. "I will see Po Po and Mama and Baba and Little Monkey." She looks at us. "I am happy and sad."

Around seven, it starts snowing. At first it looks like flurries just blowing around, but the next time we look out, it's sticking. "Maybe we'll have a snow day again tomorrow," Ken says, cupping his hands around his eyes.

"In China, we have snowstorms and dust storms, but we do not cancel school."

"Good thing I don't live in China," Ken says, looking outside for the hundredth time.

The TV says there is a winter storm warning in effect until tomorrow morning. They are expecting eight to ten inches by daybreak.

We make a big bowl of popcorn and sit around the living room watching the weather channel. Mom and

Dad are both home, and so are Ken and Kaylee and Andee and Fan. When the popcorn's gone, we play with the small rice bags. Mom is pretty good at it, but Dad throws them too high and drops everything. Fan says her dad is not very good either. "I think this is not a father's game," she says.

Ken says we all have to wear our pajamas inside out to make absolutely sure that we have a snow day. Andee and Fan and I think that's crazy, but we do it anyway, just in case. We decide to spread sleeping bags on the floor of my room and sleep all in a row as if we're camping.

"This is funny," Fan says.

"Camping without a tent," Andee says.

I take a stack of picture books off my shelf, and we take turns reading them out loud. I pick *The Little Engine That Could*. Fan reads *The Snowy Day*. Andee picks *Chrysanthemum*. And then we are too tired to keep our eyes open.

❄ ❄ ❄

As soon as I wake up, I can tell the room is strangely bright. I look outside, and snow is covering everything. I go down to the computer, and sure enough, all Cincinnati schools have been canceled.

Ken is out the door even before breakfast, shaking snow off the branches and throwing snowballs at the basketball hoop. We bundle up and head out.

"I love the way snow transforms everything," Andee says, looking up at the elm tree.

"Me too," I say. "And I love the way it smells." We breathe deeply.

"Everything is clean now," Fan says.

The snow is the heavy, wet kind, and we decide to see if we can build an igloo. I get a cardboard box from the basement to make snow bricks, and we stack them to make the walls, moving them closer together as the walls get higher. We leave a little opening at the top like a skylight. Then we build snow chairs inside and sit down to rest.

"I can't believe that you're leaving so soon," Andee says. "Do you think that in China you could go back to high school?"

Fan shakes her head. "If you stop school in China, you cannot start again."

"Will you work at the hotel?"

"I think so. Maybe now since I know English better, I can go to a short course so I can get a certificate and I can earn more money."

"If you could do whatever you wanted, what would you do?" Andee asks.

"This is impossible," Fan says, looking annoyed.

Andee persists. "But if you could."

Fan's face relaxes. "I want to be a teacher so I can teach poetry."

"I like to read poems," Andee says. "But I don't like to analyze them." She takes a lick of snow. "I used to think I'd like to be a jeweler." She pulls up the sleeve of her jacket to look at the seashell bracelet. "Or a fashion designer. But now I'm not sure."

"Me either," I say. "I used to want to work with little kids. But ever since we got Kaylee, I've changed my mind."

Fan picks up a handful of snow, throws it up, and watches it land on our igloo floor. "We cannot know what will happen in our future," she says.

"But we can still plan," Andee says. She looks at me. "Maybe we will go live in China."

"Then you can both visit me every day," Fan says, smiling.

Chapter Sixteen

Choosing Gifts

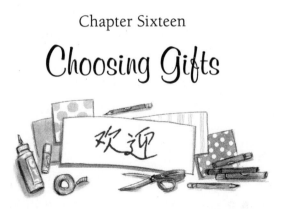

Two weeks before Fan is going to leave, Mom takes us shopping to buy gifts for Fan's family and friends in China. Ken picks out a Lego set for Fan's brother. He tells Fan that next time she comes to Cincinnati, she should bring him along. "I'm tired of so many sisters," he says.

For Fan's parents, we get jackets that say *Cincinnati* across the back. And for her friends, she picks out T-shirts and baseball hats. The only person we don't have a gift for is her grandma.

"How about a scarf?" Mom suggests.

"In the countryside she does not wear a scarf," Fan says.

"What does she like?" I ask.

Fan considers. "She likes flowers. She grows them in the yard, and then she brings them into the house to put in a cup on the table." Fan's voice breaks. "I don't know what she does now, without Gong Gong."

"When spring comes, the flowers will grow," Mom says. "Maybe we can get her something for the yard."

Finally we decide on a pair of hand pruners with orange handles, and also a glass vase with specks of different colors like glitter all around.

"Very beautiful," Fan says, holding the vase up to catch the light.

❄ ❄ ❄

When we get home, Fan sits on the sofa with the history book, as usual. But she doesn't open it. "I finished," she says, handing me a list of twenty review questions. She has answered each one in her small, even handwriting. "The teacher will give me the test early."

"Do you want me to quiz you?" I ask.

Fan considers. "No, I think I am ready." She puts the book down on the coffee table, stands up, and stretches.

"What do you want to do?" I ask.

Fan looks at the clock. "I think we can cook dinner."

We go into the kitchen. "What should we make?" I ask.

Fan opens the freezer, which is full of packages of meat and vegetables. "We can make my mother's dumplings. Remember, you tasted them in my home."

My mouth waters just thinking about the chewy dough and salty meat. "What should we do first?"

Fan gets out the flour and dumps some into a bowl without measuring it. She adds a little water from the faucet. "We make the dough." Fan shows me how to

 take little balls of dough and press them flat in the palm of my hand. Then we defrost a package of pork in the microwave and mix it with soy sauce, sesame oil, salt, pepper, and garlic. We put a little meat into the middle of each circle of dough and pinch it closed. We talk and laugh and fold dumplings for over an hour until we have more than one hundred.

"I think we can invite Andee's family," Fan says, looking at the cookie sheets covered with dumplings.

Andee and her parents love the dumplings. Her father eats so many that he says he will have to fast for the next three days.

"But first let's get ice cream," my dad says, patting his stomach. We pile into two cars and head to Graeter's.

❋ ❋ ❋

"I wish I could take ice cream back for my family," Fan says. "We have ice cream in China, but Graeter's is better."

"When they come to visit," Andee says, "we can bring them to Graeter's."

I think Fan will say that it is impossible for her family to come to America. But then she says, "Mama will chose vanilla."

"What about your brother?" Ken asks.

"He likes chocolate," she says.

"Just like me," Ken says, taking a big lick.

Chapter Seventeen

A Surprise Party

$\mathcal{A}$ndee and I decide to have a surprise going-away dinner for Fan. We invite the volleyball team, Teacher Zhao, the Sylvesters, Mr. Freeman, and Camille.

"What should we have?" Andee asks.

"Fan still likes Chinese food more than American food."

"But she told me the other day that she's going to miss American pizza when she goes home."

"Really? I thought she hated cheese," I say.

"Not anymore," Andee says.

We decide to have seaweed soup, pizza, salad, and ice cream sandwiches for dessert.

A girl on the volleyball team invited Fan over for the afternoon, so Andee and I have time to get ready and work on our gift. Mom makes seaweed soup, and Andee's mom is bringing the pizza. Andee and I set the table with red place mats and red napkins for Chinese New Year. Then we go into the den to work on the scrapbook we are making of Fan's stay in Cincinnati. On the first page, we put a photo of Fan on the day she arrived with her big suitcase and her orange T-shirt.

"Fan looks different now," Andee says.

I stare at the photo. Her face looks scared and tired. "You're right. Now she looks . . . happier."

Above the photo, Andee draws a little globe with China on the front, and a tiny airplane. On page two, we put a photo of Andee's family and mine.

"Now what?" Andee asks.

"Fenwick High," I say.

We have a page for the volleyball team and a page for CAT. Then we make a collage with pictures of some of the new foods Fan tried in the United States, including peanut butter ice cream. Andee makes a page with

things she saved
from Florida, like
the menu at the
Palm restaurant
and the Disney
World passes.
We spend hours as-

sembling the whole book. Each time we
think we're done, we think of things we forgot.

"Let's put in a scrap of fabric from the rice bags."

"And a picture of Jing."

Finally we wrap the scrapbook in blue and white
tissue paper, since those are Fenwick's colors, and tie
it with a blue ribbon.

Andee puts the gift in the middle of the table. "When
Fan first got here, I was counting the days until her
visit would be over." Andee rubs her face. "And now I
can't believe she's leaving early."

Everyone hides behind the sofa and the living room
chairs, except Jing, who insists on sitting right in the

middle of the floor. As soon as Fan opens the door, we jump out and yell, "SURPRISE!"

At first, Fan doesn't understand that the party is for her.

"It's called a surprise party," I say.

She starts to say something in English, switches to Chinese, and then goes back to English again. "I cannot talk in any language," she says, laughing.

Everyone loves the soup and the pizza. Camille brings a cake that says *Zai jian* and *Goodbye* in blue frosting. Fan takes pictures of everything.

Jing follows Kaylee everywhere she goes.

"I am the big sister," Kaylee says, pointing to herself. She marches around the living room with Jing right behind her.

Ms. Sylvester laughs. "Kaylee is the *jie jie*," she says, looking at Fan to make sure that she pronounced it right.

Fan gets lots of presents, including a Fenwick banner, new socks, and a Cincinnati mug. She saves the scrapbook for last, removing the wrapping paper carefully so it won't tear. She looks at each page, smiling at the memories.

"I will keep putting pages," she says.

"Until you come back—with your brother," Ken says.

After everyone else has gone home, Fan and Andee and I go up to my room. We play cards and listen to songs on the radio. Fan yawns. Mom comes in and takes a picture of the three of us. Then we get into our pajamas and brush our teeth. Nobody wants to sleep in the bed, so we curl up in sleeping bags on the floor.

"What are you going to do when you get home?" Andee asks.

"If we can pay for the tickets, we will take a long train trip to the countryside to see Po Po. It will be strange to be in the house without Gong Gong." Fan looks up. "I will miss Gong Gong."

"It will be strange in my house without you," Andee says softly.

❄ ❄ ❄

Fan falls asleep quickly, but Andee and I decide to go downstairs to make a goodbye card. We sit together in our den with the light shining on the table. "What should we put on the front?" Andee asks.

"How about the three of us?" I say.

We cut three figures out of paper scraps. One is tall with brown curly hair. Two are short with straight black hair. Underneath we write our names.

"What about inside?" Andee asks.

I think of the usual things people write in farewell cards, like *We hope to see you soon* or *Thanks for coming,* but nothing sounds right for Fan.

"I think I remember how to write *goodbye* in Chinese," Andee says, taking the card and writing the characters for *zai jian* above the picture. But the inside of the card is empty.

"Fan likes poems," I say.

On scratch paper, we list everything we can think of that Fan did in America. Then we alternate writing the lines of a goodbye poem. When it's done, I copy it over in my best handwriting, and Andee makes little drawings around the border. Then we put the card into an envelope, lick it shut, and write *Jie Jie,* sister, on the front. In parentheses I write: (To open on the plane.)

Epilogue

Three Sisters

Jet lag and ice cream,
Baby swings and Legos,
Badminton and volleyball,
We miss you, Fan.

Hot sun and swirling leaves,
Vocabulary words and rice bags,
Snow days and dumplings,
We miss you, Fan.

Disney World and seashells,
History and poetry,
Fire and ashes,
We miss you, Fan.

Xie xie and thank you,
Different and the same,
Memories shared
By sisters.
Love,
    Anna and Andee